Winnie the Pooh

Playing Games

Adapted from a story by Mary Hogan

Illustrations by John Kurtz

Pooh hadn't traveled very far along a rambling path in the Hundred-Acre Wood when he heard a familiar voice. And with a sudden bounce and a bump, Pooh found himself looking right up at Tigger.

"Hiya, Buddy Bear!" said Tigger. "Terrifically bouncety day for a bounce, don't ya agree? Hoo-hoo-hoo!"

"A little too bouncety for a bear," said Pooh with a sigh.

"Too bouncety?" asked Tigger. "Is that possible?"

"All tiggers love bouncing," explained Pooh. "But not all pooh bears love being bounced."

"Most interestin'," said Tigger, looking quite surprised.

"Good manners are mostly about looking at things from someone else's point of view," said Pooh.

"Well, how do things look down there?" Tigger asked Pooh, still sitting on top of his round friend.

"Kind of orange and . . . stripedy," said Pooh.

"Say, you're lookin' at things exactackily like a tigger!" cried Tigger. "But you're not the onliest one with manners. Let me help ya up."

"Thank you, Tigger," said Pooh.

"Furthermost, Pooh Bear, I am most sorrily sorry for this and all the tiggerific future bounces sure an' certain to come your way," offered Tigger.

"Oh bother," said Pooh. "I mean, thank you, Tigger."

"How 'bout I make it up to ya with a game o' Pooh Sticks," suggested Tigger. "I've found some extry-speediferous sticks just right for racin'."

"All right," agreed Pooh.

Tigger shared his new sticks with Pooh.

The friends tossed their sticks off the side of a nearby bridge. Then they raced to the other side to see whose stick would be the first to pass under the bridge.

"Pooh Sticks are what tiggers do best," bragged Tigger. Then he looked at his friend. "Pooh bears are pretty terrifical, too," he added.

"There's my stick!" said Pooh happily. "I win!"

"Let's play again," said Tigger.

Tigger loved playing Pooh Sticks, but he loved it most when he won. So when Pooh said, "Ready . . . set . . ." Tigger threw his stick.

"And throw!" finished Pooh, and threw in his own stick.

Soon Tigger's stick appeared at the other side of the bridge. It was ahead of Pooh's stick, but Tigger didn't quite feel like a winner.

"Let's play that one again," said Tigger. "My stick had a bit of a twitchy feel about it."

"Okay," agreed Pooh. He had thought Tigger's toss looked a little twitchy (in a there-it-goes-and-I-haven't-quite-called-"throw"-yet kind of way). But Pooh hadn't wanted to say so.

The friends tossed sticks again, right at the same time. Pooh's came out ahead again.

"Good goin' there," Tigger said, giving his friend's paw a shake, but looking a little down around the whiskers all the same.

Pooh looked at his remaining sticks. One had a bright green bud on it. "I think this is a lucky sort of Pooh Stick," said Pooh. "Do you want to use this one?"

"Why, thanks, Buddy Bear," said Tigger, cheering right up. And soon Tigger's lucky stick had won the very next race.

"Hoo-hoo-hoo!" hooted Tigger. "Playin' fair an' square is what tiggers— and poohs—do best."